KILLER KOALAS
FROM OUTER SPACE

and Lots of Other Very Bad Stuff
that Will Make Your Brain Explode!

KILLER KOALAS FROM OUTER SPACE

and Lots of Other Very Bad Stuff
that Will Make Your Brain Explode!

by
**Andy
Griffiths**

illustrations by
**Terry
Denton**

Killer Koalas from Outer Space

Killer koalas from outer space:
They look cute and cuddly,
but they'll rip off your face!

They come here disguised
as cute marsupials,
but they're really face-ripping
extraterrestrials!

So, if I were you, from this place I would race
before those koalas (with unseemly haste)
get out their claws and
RIP OFF YOUR FACE!

WE REGRET TO INFORM YOU

THAT KILLER KOALAS

FROM OUTER SPACE

HAVE LANDED ON EARTH

AND ARE RUNNING AROUND

RIPPING EVERYBODY'S

FACES OFF....

RIP!!

RIP!!

MORE BAD NEWS

AS IT COMES TO HAND.

RIP!!

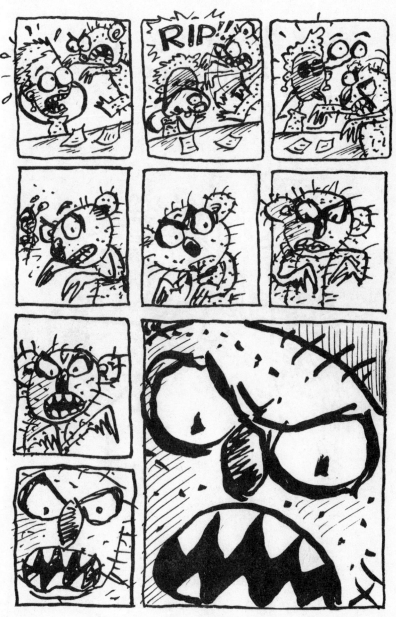

THE END

Very Bad Mary, Quite Contrary

Very Bad Mary, quite contrary,
how does your garden grow?
With poison ivy, prickles, and thistles,
and spiky weeds all in a row?

Little Willy

Eating more than he was able,
Willy died at the breakfast table.
"Please, Mama," said little Meg.
"May I have his other egg?"

Bad Mommy and Daddy and the Volcano

THE END

The Old Woman
Who Lived in a Poo

There was an old woman
who lived in a poo.

She had so many flies,
she didn't know what to do!

She gave them some broth
and put them to bed.

Then sprayed them
with fly spray
until they were dead.

The Very Bad Ant and the Big Red Shiny Space Rocket

Once upon a time, there was an ant. It *looked* like an ordinary ant, but it wasn't. It was a very bad ant.

And the very bad ant
went along the
ground and came to
a stick.
And the very bad ant
went up the stick. And
the very bad ant went over the stick.
And the very bad ant went down the stick.

And the very bad ant went along the ground
and came to a blade of grass.
And the very bad ant went up the blade of grass.
And the very bad ant went over the blade of grass.
And the very bad ant went down the blade of grass.

And then it stopped.

And then it started again.

And the very bad ant went along the ground
and came to a big red shiny space rocket.
And the very bad ant went up
the big red shiny space rocket.
And the very bad ant
went *into* the big red shiny space rocket.

And the very bad ant pressed the START button!

WHOOSH! went the big red shiny space rocket as it blasted off into space.

"COME BACK WITH OUR BIG RED SHINY SPACE ROCKET!" shouted the astronauts. But it was no use. The very bad ant couldn't hear them above the roar of the rocket, and even if it could have, it would have kept on flying anyway because, as I think I have already mentioned, it was a *very bad* ant.

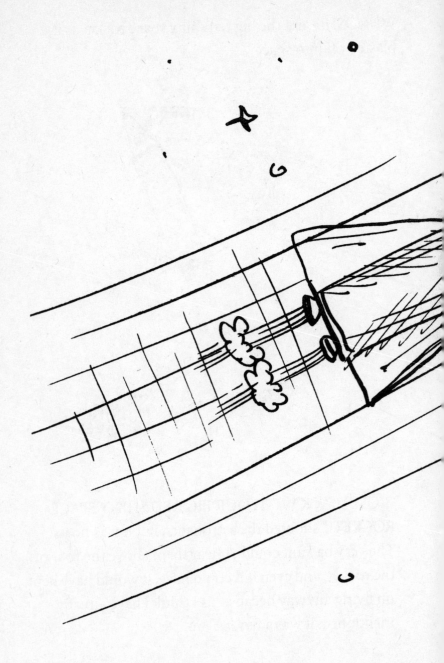

And the very bad ant went past the moon.

And the very bad ant went past Venus.

And the very bad ant went past Mercury and
headed straight toward the sun, which was
a very dangerous thing to do because the sun
is very, very hot. Especially when you get really
close to it.

But do you think the very bad ant cared?
No, of course not.
It didn't even have its seat belt fastened
or its space helmet on!

The very bad ant just flew the big red shiny space
rocket straight into the sun and was burned to death.
Which wasn't very nice. But not very surprising,
because it was a bad ant. A *very* bad ant.

THE END

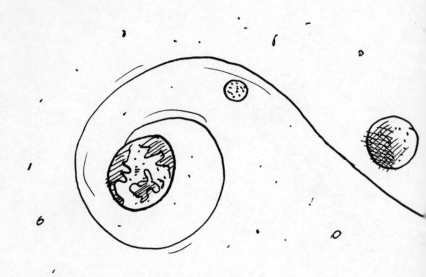

Very Bad Koala Riddles

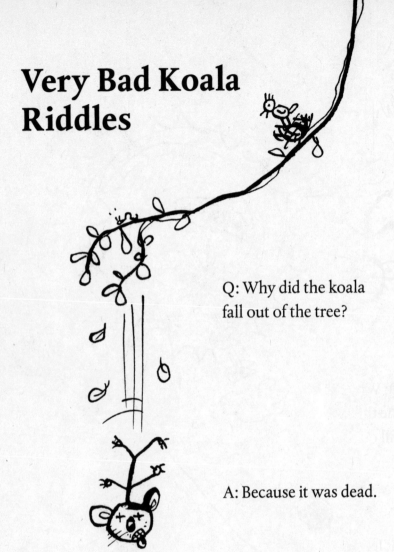

Q: Why did the koala
fall out of the tree?

A: Because it was dead.

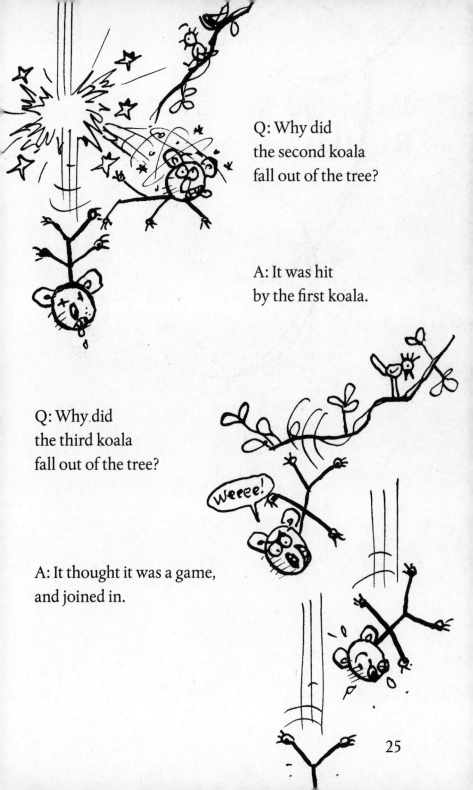

Q: Why did
the second koala
fall out of the tree?

A: It was hit
by the first koala.

Q: Why did
the third koala
fall out of the tree?

Weeee!

A: It thought it was a game,
and joined in.

25

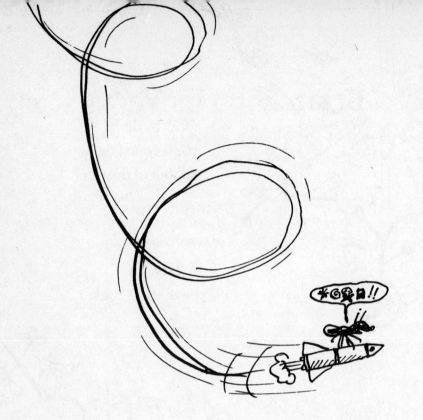

Brian and His Very Bad Idea

THE END

The Three Bad Guys
and the Very Bad Idea

Once upon a time, there were three bad guys:
a big bad guy, a medium-sized bad guy, and
a little bad guy.

One day, the three bad guys were sitting around in
their clubhouse thinking up bad stuff to do when
the big bad guy said, "Hey, I've got a very bad idea!
Let's not wash our hands after going to the toilet!"

"That *is* a very bad idea!" said the medium-sized bad guy, "and let's *also* not wash them after picking our noses!"

"Yeah!" said the little bad guy. "And let's *especially* not wash them after touching pets and other animals!"

And the three bad guys all high-fived each other and agreed that not washing their hands was a *very bad idea* and they began not washing their hands immediately.

As it turned out, the three bad guys were right; not washing their hands *was* a very bad idea because it wasn't long before their hands were covered in really nasty germs that crawled up their arms, invaded their bodies, and caused sniffles, rashes, fevers, coughing, vomiting, diarrhoea, hepatitis A, hepatitis B, halitosis, tuberculosis, myxomatosis, supercalifragilisticexpialidosis, and tummyache . . . all of which made the three bad guys feel *very* bad indeed!

THE END

Very Rude Animals

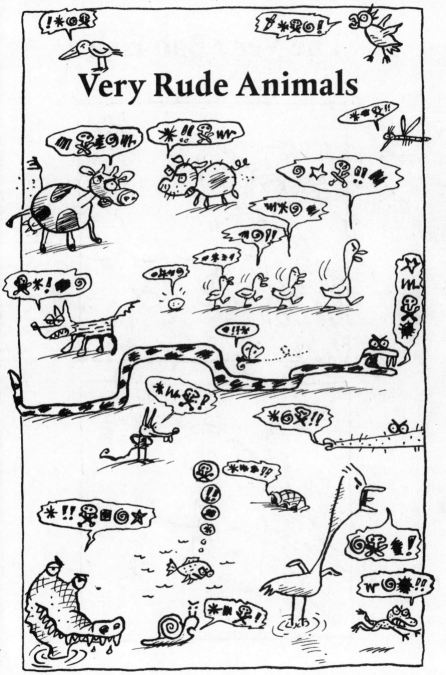

The Very Bad Fish

THE END

The Dog that Fell Apart

Once upon a time, there was a dog.

One day, the dog's tail fell off.

The next day, his legs fell off.

The next day, his nose fell off.

The next day, his ears fell off.

The next day, his head fell off.

The next day was Tuesday.

THE END

THE END

Very Bad Farmer Riddles

Q: What did the farmer say when he couldn't find his tractor?

A: "Where's my tractor?"

Q: What did the farmer say when he found his tractor?

A: "There's my tractor!"

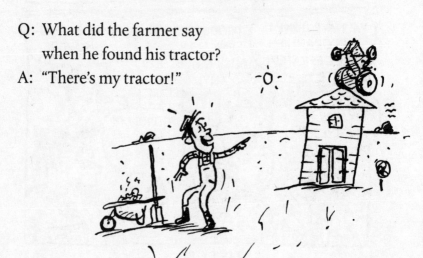

Q: What do you call a farmer with
a tractor on his head?
A: Dead.

Very Bad Invention No. 1: The Non-flush Toilet

Very Bad Invention No. 2:
Non-elastic Underpants

Nobody Likes Me

Nobody likes me, everybody hates me,
think I'm gonna eat some worms.
First you chop their heads off,
then you squeeze their guts out.
Ooh, what a horrible mess . . . YUCK!

Bad Macdonald

Bad Macdonald had a really stinky farm,
ee-i-ee-i *pee-uw!*
And on that farm, he had a dead pig
with its guts coming out,
ee-i-ee-i *pee-uw!*
With pig guts here,
and pig guts there.
Here some guts!
There some guts!
Everywhere, some pig guts!
Bad Macdonald had a really stinky farm,
ee-i-ee-i *pee-uw!*

Bad Macdonald had a really stinky farm,
ee-i-ee-i *pee-uw!*
And on that farm, he had a dead cow
with its guts coming out,
ee-i-ee-i *pee-uw!*
With cow guts here,
and cow guts there.
Here some guts!
There some guts!
Everywhere, some cow guts!
Bad Macdonald had a really stinky farm,
ee-i-ee-i *pee-uw!*

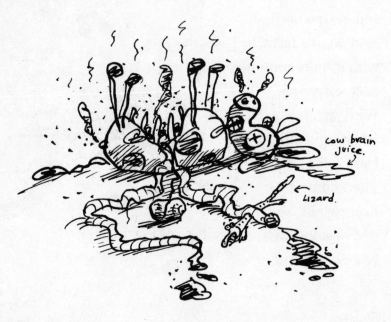

cow brain
juice.

Lizard.

Bad Macdonald had a really stinky farm,
ee-i-ee-i *pee-uw!*
And on that farm, he had a dead horse
with its guts coming out,
ee-i-ee-i *pee-uw!*
With horse guts here,
and horse guts there.
Here some guts!
There some guts!
Everywhere, some horse guts!
Bad Macdonald had a really stinky farm,
ee-i-ee-i *pee-uw!*

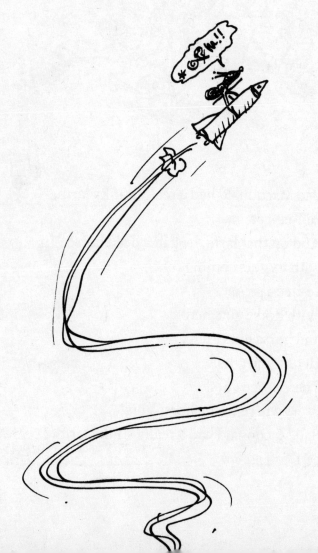

The Boy Who Ate Dead Flies

ONE DAY, A LITTLE BOY WAS SITTING BY A WINDOW WHEN HE FOUND A DEAD FLY.

Mom, can I eat this dead fly?

Don't be silly, dear, that's disgusting! You'll make yourself sick.

BUT THE BOY DIDN'T LISTEN TO HIS MOTHER.

I'm going to do it anyway.

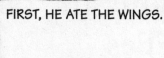

THEN, HE ATE THE EYES.

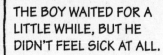

THEN, HE ATE THE BODY.

THE BOY WAITED FOR A
LITTLE WHILE, BUT HE
DIDN'T FEEL SICK AT ALL.

SO, THE BOY ATE ANOTHER
DEAD FLY.

AND ANOTHER . . .

WINGS BURST OUT OF HIS BACK.

HIS EYES BULGED AND HIS NOSE GREW . . .

AND BEFORE HE KNEW IT, HE WAS HOVERING ABOVE THE GROUND!

THEN, HE TOOK OFF AROUND THE ROOM.

HE LOOPED THE LOOP.

HE CIRCLED THE LIGHT.

THE END

Very Stupid Riddles

Q: Why couldn't the cat drink its milk?
A: Because it didn't have a face.

Q: What's red and not there?
A: No tomato.

Q: What's brown and looks out the window?

A: A poo on stilts.

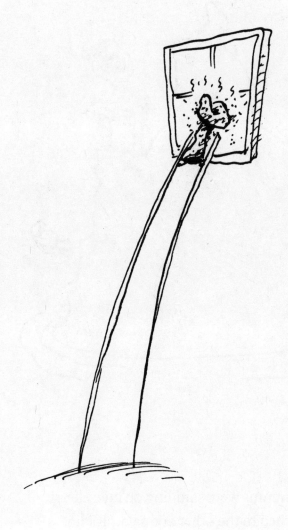

Very Bad Penguin Joke

Two penguins were standing on an iceberg.
One turned to the other and said, "Radio."

The Very Bad Road

BAD
ROAD
AHEAD

65

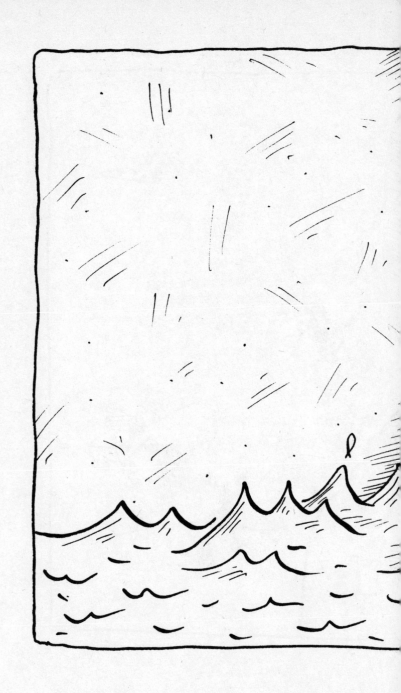

THE END

The Sad Bad Bad-man

Once upon a time,
    there was a sad bad bad-man.
The sad bad bad-man was sad
    because he was bad
      at being bad.

So, the sad bad bad-man
went to sad bad bad-man's school

where they taught
        sad bad bad-men
how to be good at being
        good bad-men,
instead of being good at being
        sad bad bad-men.

And the sad bad bad-man stopped being sad
 and became glad
because he learned how to be a good bad-man
 who was good at being bad,
 instead of bad at being bad.

In fact,

the ex-sad bad bad-man

was so good at being bad

that he became

the gladdest ex-sad bad bad-man

in the history of

sad bad bad-men

who stopped being sad bad bad-men

and became

glad good bad-men.

THE END

Mud Brown
and the Seven Slobs

Once upon a slime, there was a disgusting princess
called Mud Brown. She lived in a stinking bog
with seven slobs called Stinky, Filthy, Snotty,
Messy, Grubby, Sloppy, and Robert.

Mud Brown and the seven slobs ate dirt, put mud
in their underpants, sneezed in each other's faces,
shoved handfuls of worms in their ears, and never
EVER brushed their teeth.

One day, an unhandsome prince called Prince
Poopy-pants came riding through the forest on a filthy
warthog and saw Mud Brown and the seven slobs
having a wild mud fight.

Prince Poopy-pants looked at Mud Brown's filthy clothes, dirty face, matted hair, and ears full of nasty wriggling worms, and fell in love with her at once.

He leapt from his warthog and waded into the bog
toward her. "You are the dirtiest, most perfectly
despicable princess I have ever laid my beady,
bloodshot eyes on!" he said. "Will you marry me?"

Mud Brown scooped up a big handful of mud and slammed it right in the prince's face. "Of course I will," she said. "I've been waiting all my life for someone as unhandsome, unappealing, and unhygienic as you!"

Prince Poopy-pants and Mud Brown embraced and kissed but, unfortunately, as neither of them had ever cleaned their teeth in their entire lives, the combined stench of their terrible breath formed a cloud so toxic that it not only killed them both, but also Stinky, Filthy, Snotty, Messy, Grubby, Sloppy, and Robert. And nobody lived ever after.

THE END

Mommy, Mommy!

Son: Mommy, Mommy! What's a
   werewolf?
Mom: Shut up and comb your face!

Son: Mommy, Mommy! Are we really
   vampires?
Mom: Shut up and drink your soup
   before it clots!

Son: Mommy, Mommy! I'm scared of
   zombies!
Mom: Shut up and eat your brains while
   they're still warm!

THE END

83

The Very Bad Giraffe

THE END

The Very Bad Dentist

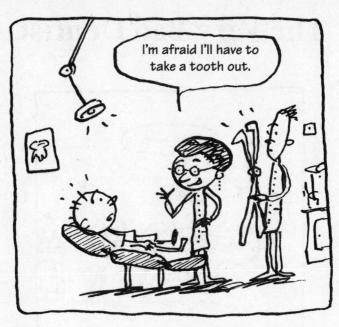

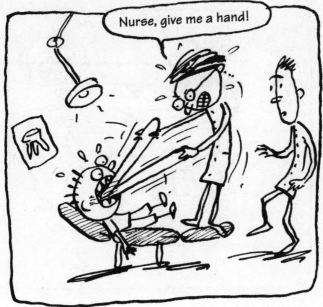

THE END

Very Bad Tree Riddles

Q: Why did the man
cut down the tree?

A: Because it was there.

Q: Why didn't the man
cut down the tree?

A: Because it
wasn't there.

Q: Why did the tree
cut down the man?

A: Because
it was a bad tree.

Brian and His Very, Very Bad Idea

THE END

The Girl Who Slammed Doors

There once was a girl who slammed doors
from morning to night without pause.
   She slammed them so hard
    that the rooms fell apart,
and all that was left were the floors.

Very Bad Hippo Joke

Two hippos are in a swamp
with water up to their eyes.
One looks at the other and says,
"I don't know why, but I keep thinking
it's Tuesday."

The Boy Who Forgot His Head Because It Wasn't Screwed On

Once upon a time, there was a very forgetful boy. He would forget to do his chores. He would forget to do his homework. And sometimes, he would even forget to put his pants on before he went to school!

You forgot your pants!

"Honestly!" his mother would say, shaking her head. "You'd forget your head if it wasn't screwed on!"

One day, the boy said to himself,
"I wonder if my head really *is* screwed on?"
The boy put his hands over his ears
and twisted his head to the right.
It moved a little.

He gave another twist.
It moved a little more.

He gave it one more twist and,
to his surprise, his head came
completely off his body.

"Cool!" said the boy. "My head really does screw on . . . and off!" And he screwed it on.

And off.

And on.

And off.

And on.

And off.

He was about to screw it on again when he heard his best friend calling from outside and he ran off to play, completely forgetting to screw his head back on, just as his mother had predicted.

The boy's head sat
on the table in front
of the window where the
boy had left it. Pretty
soon, however, the wind
started to blow and . . .

the head rolled off the
table and onto the floor.

It bounced down
the stairs,

and out the front door.

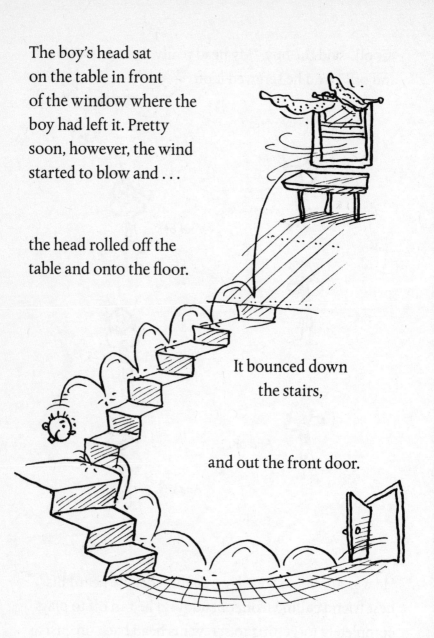

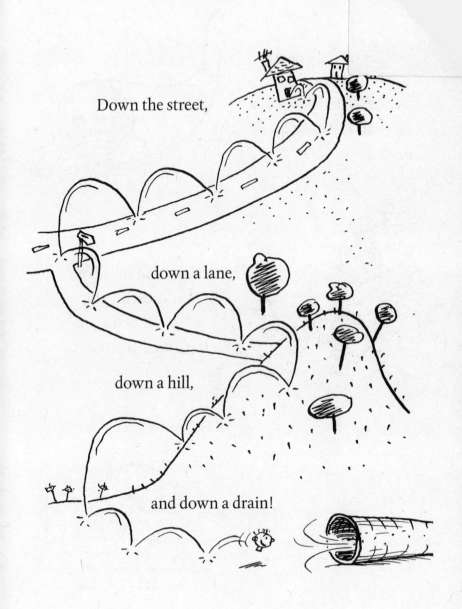

Down the street,

down a lane,

down a hill,

and down a drain!

Along a dark
and slimy pipe,
past frogs and toads
and rats that bite!

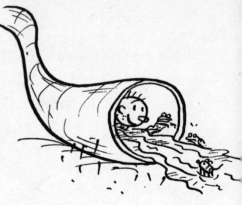

The head rolled on
until, eventually,
it slid out of the pipe
and splashed into the sea . . .

where it was swallowed
by a fish . . .

which was swallowed
by a *very* big fish . . .

which was swallowed
by a very, *very* big fish . . .

which was swallowed by
a very, very, very *small* fish . . .

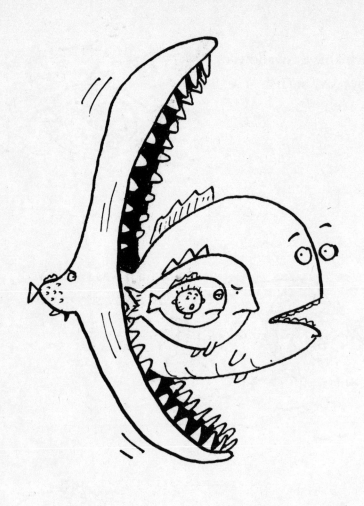

with a very, very, very *big* mouth!

And

the

very,

very, very

small fish

with the

very,

very,

very

big mouth

was caught by

a fisherman,

who took it home,
cut it open,
and out rolled
the boy's head!

So, the fisherman did what he did with all
the interesting things he found inside the fish
he caught: He put it on eBay and, after a
furious bidding war, it was bought by a
little old lady who cleaned it, polished it up,
and used it as a bowling ball.

As for the boy,
don't feel too sorry for him.
He soon forgot he'd ever had
a head and lived happily—
and headlessly—
ever after.

THE END

Tarzan the Monkey Man

Tarzan the monkey man,
swinging on a rubber band.
Along came Superman
and kicked him in the garbage can!

The Adventures of
the Dog Poo Family

PART 1

THE END

The Adventures of the Dog Poo Family

PART 2

THE END

The Adventures of the Dog Poo Family

PART 3

THE END

The Very Bad Holiday

DAY 1: STEP IN DOG POO

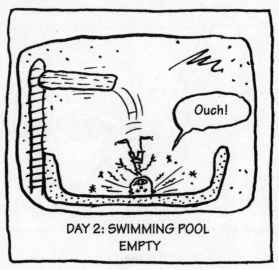

DAY 2: SWIMMING POOL
EMPTY

DAY 3: SWIMMING POOL
FULL OF DOG POO

DAY 4: CHASED BY LIONS

DAY 5: CHASED BY DOG POO

DAY 6: ICE CREAM FALLS
OFF STICK

THE END

The Very Bad Guide to Good and Bad

Cute fluffy kittens
BAD!

Zombie kittens
GOOD!

Cute fluffy koalas
BAD!

ARRGHH!

Killer koalas who rip off your face
GOOD!

Helping old people cross the road
BAD!

Helping old people rob banks
GOOD!

Giving people presents
BAD!

Cough!
Cough!

Giving people germs
GOOD!

Good books
BAD!

Bad books
GOOD!

Little Bad Riding Hood

Once upon a time, there was a bad little girl called Little Bad Riding Hood.

One day,
her mother said to her,
"Little Bad Riding Hood,
your grandmother is
very sick.

Would you
do me a favor
and take her
this basket of food,
drink,
and vital medicine
without which,
she will surely die?"

And Little Bad Riding Hood said,

"No."

THE END

Peter, Peter, Junk food Eater

Peter, Peter, junk food eater
guzzled lemonade by the liter.
gobbled jelly beans by the ton
ate ice cream cakes and sticky buns.

He began to grow and swell
and was not looking very well.
He drank a milk shake to quench his thirst.
He groaned,
   and burped,
     and then
   he burst.

Bad Daddy and the Pencil Sharpener

THE END

Very Bad
Knock-knock Jokes

Knock knock!
Who's there?
Poo-poo.
Poo-poo who?
Poo-poo wee-wee.

Knock knock!
Who's there?
Poo-poo wee-wee.
Poo-poo wee-wee who?
Poo-poo wee-wee poo-poo wee-wee.

Knock knock!
Who's there?
Alice.
Alice who?
Alice Poo-poo wee-wee poo-poo wee-wee.

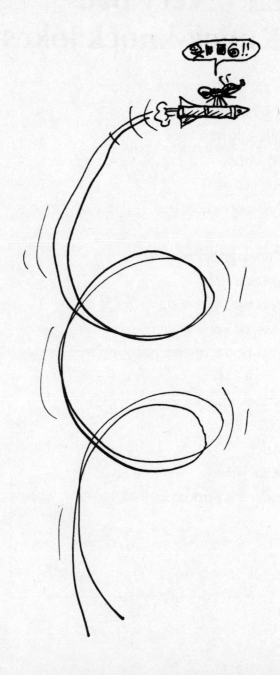

Brian and His Very, Very Very Bad Idea

THE END

The Very Bad Builder

Once upon a time,
there was a very bad builder.

Everybody would say to him,
"Can you fix it?"
and he would say,
"No,
I can't."

THE END

Badword Puzzle

CLUES

Across
1. Not good (3)
2. Wicked (3)
3. Naughty (3)
5. DAB backwards (3)
6. Shoddy (3)
8. Faulty (3)
9. Imperfect (3)
10. Terrible (3)
11. Off or sour (3)
13. Disobedient (3)
14. Harmful (3)
16. Rotten (3)
17. Putrid (3)
18. Good-for-nothing (3)

Down
1. Evil (3)
3. Rhymes with sad (3)
4. Dreadful (3)
5. Rude (3)
6. Nasty (3)
7. Gross (3)
8. Offensive (3)
10. Misbehaved (3)
11. Useless (3)
12. Worthless (3)
13. Vile (3)
14. Atrocious (3)
15. Sinful (3)
16. Abominable (3)
17. Despicable (3)

Solution:

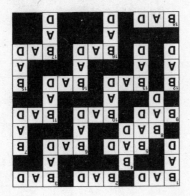

The Very Bad Story

Once upon a time, things were bad. Then, things got very bad. And just when everybody thought things couldn't possibly get any badder, they did.

They got very, very bad.

THE END

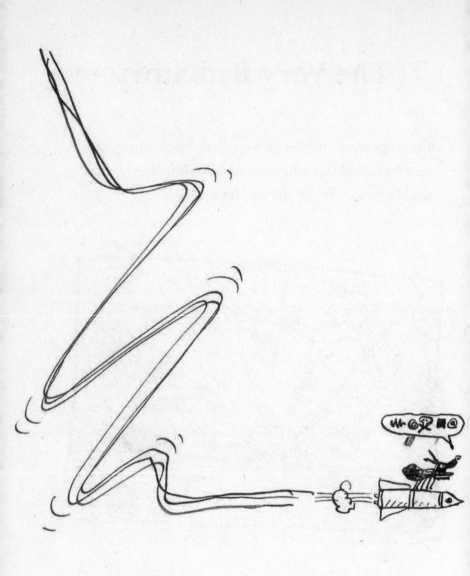

The Very, Very Bad Story

Once upon a time, things were very, very bad. And just when everybody thought things couldn't possibly get any badder, they did. They got twice as bad.

Then they got three times as bad.

Then they got four thousand, eight hundred, and seventy-three and five-sixteenths badder still.

THE END

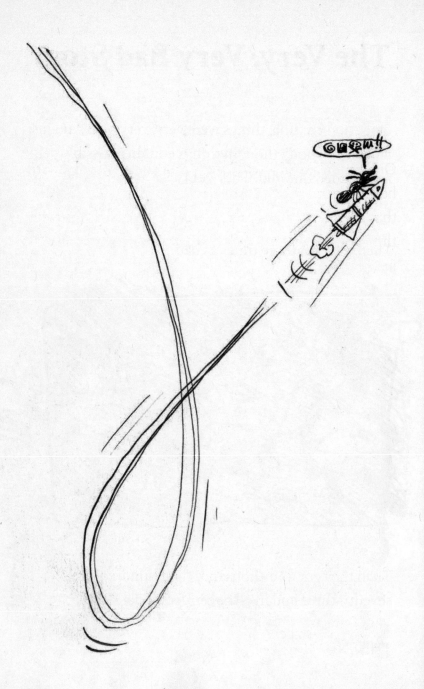

The Very, Very, Very Bad Story

Once upon a time, things were four thousand, eight hundred, and seventy-three and five-sixteenths badder than the time things were three times as bad as the time things were twice as bad as the time when they were just very, very bad.

In fact, things were SO bad that it made all the previous bad days seem like the good old days, and the memory of those good old bad days made everybody cry and feel very sorry for themselves and feel even badder than they already did.

But eventually, people started saying, "Hey, we can't just sit around crying all day and feeling bad. We should try to fix things and make everything good again."

So everybody got up, wiped their tears away, stopped feeling sorry for themselves, and tried to make things good again.

But it was no use. The more they tried to make things good again, the badder things got. Things just got badder and

badder and badder and badder and badder and badder
and badder and badder and badder and badder and
badder and badder and badder and badder and badder
and badder and badder and badder and badder and
badder and badder and badder and badder and badder
and badder and badder and badder and badder and
badder and badder and badder and badder and badder
and badder and badder and badder and badder and
badder and badder and badder and badder and badder
and badder and badder and badder and badder and
badder and badder and badder and badder and badder
and badder and badder and badder and badder and
badder and badder and badder and badder and badder
and badder and badder and badder and badder and
badder and badder and badder and badder and badder
and badder and badder and badder and badder and
badder and badder and badder and badder and badder
and badder and badder and badder and badder and
badder and badder and badder and badder and badder
and badder and badder and badder and badder and
badder and badder and badder and badder and badder
and badder and badder and badder and badder and
badder and badder and badder and badder and badder
and badder and badder and badder and badder and

badder and badder and badder and badder and badder
and badder and badder and badder and badder and
badder and badder and badder and badder and badder
and badder and badder and badder and badder and
badder and badder and badder and badder and badder
and badder and badder and badder and badder and
badder and badder and badder and badder and badder
and badder and badder and badder and badder and
badder and badder and badder and badder and badder
and badder and badder and badder and badder and
badder and badder and badder and badder and badder
and badder and badder and badder and badder and
badder and badder and badder and badder and badder
and badder and badder and badder and badder and
badder and badder and badder and badder and badder
and badder and badder and badder and badder and
badder and badder and badder and badder and badder
and badder and badder and badder and badder and
badder and badder and badder and badder and badder
and badder and badder and badder and badder and
badder and badder and badder and badder and badder
and badder and badder and badder and badder and
badder and badder and badder and badder and badder
and badder and badder and badder and badder and
badder and badder and badder and badder and badder
and badder and badder and badder and badder and

badder and badder and badder and badder and badder
and badder and badder and badder and badder and
badder and badder and badder and badder and badder
and badder and badder and badder and badder and
badder and badder and badder and badder and badder
and badder and badder and badder and badder and
badder and badder and badder and badder and badder
and badder and badder and badder and badder and
badder and badder and badder and badder and badder
and badder and badder and badder and badder and
badder and badder and badder and badder and badder
and badder and badder and badder and badder and
badder and badder and badder and badder and badder
and badder and badder and badder and badder and
badder and badder and badder and badder and badder
and badder and badder and badder and badder and
badder and badder and badder and badder and badder
and badder and badder and badder and badder and
badder and badder and badder and badder and badder
and badder and badder and badder and badder and
badder and badder and badder and badder and badder
and badder and badder and badder and badder and
badder and badder and badder and badder and badder
and badder and badder and badder and badder and

badder and badder and

badder and badder and badder and badder and badder
and badder and badder and badder and badder and
badder and badder and badder and badder and badder
and badder and badder and badder and badder and
badder and badder and badder and badder and badder
and badder and badder and badder and badder and
badder and badder and badder and badder and badder
and badder and badder and badder and badder and
badder and badder and badder and badder and badder
and badder and badder and badder and badder and
badder and badder and badder and badder and badder
and badder and badder and badder and badder and
badder and badder and badder and badder and badder
and badder and badder and badder and badder and
badder and badder and badder and badder and badder
and badder and badder and badder and badder and
badder and badder and badder and badder and badder
and badder and badder and badder and badder and
badder and badder and badder and badder and badder
and badder and badder and badder and badder and
badder and badder and badder and badder and badder
and badder and badder and badder and badder and
badder and badder and badder and badder and badder
and badder and badder and badder and badder and

badder and badder.

THE END

Very Bad Plane, Ship, and Bread Van Riddles

Q: Why did the plane crash?
A: Because the pilot was a loaf of bread.

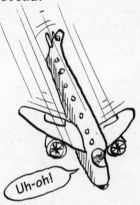

Q: Why did the ship crash?
A: Because the captain was a loaf of bread.

Q: Why did the bread van crash?

A: Accident investigators believe that it was due to a combination of factors, including high winds, icy roads, a dirty windshield, brake failure, four flat tires, and an indicator malfunction (plus the fact that the driver was a loaf of bread).

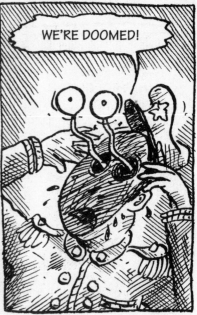

YES!

GOFISH

questions for the author

ANDY GRIFFITHS

What did you want to be when you grew up?
A rock and roll singer.

When did you realize you wanted to be a writer?
When I realized I couldn't sing.

What's your first childhood memory?
Being chased around the bath by brown blobs.

What's your most embarrassing childhood memory?
Being chased around the bath by brown blobs.

What's your favorite childhood memory?
NOT being chased around the bath by brown blobs.

As a young person, who did you look up to most?
Wile E. Coyote from the Road Runner cartoon. He never gave up.

What was your worst subject in school?
Math. If only two plus two equaled five, I would have been a genius.

What was your best subject in school?
English. What's so hard about spelling hipppapotamuss?

What was your first job?
Cleaning up my bedroom. I got fired after my first day.

How did you celebrate publishing your first book?
I got a tattoo: one of the fish from Dr. Seuss's *One Fish Two Fish Red Fish Blue Fish.*

Where do you write your books?
Wherever I am . . . usually in an exercise book.

Where do you find inspiration for your writing?
In dangerous and/or embarrassing situations.

Which of your characters is most like you?
Andy Griffiths from the Just! series. It's largely autobiographical.

When you finish a book, who reads it first?
My wife, Jill.

Are you a morning person or a night owl?
I love getting up at 6:00 AM and going for a long run.

What's your idea of the best meal ever?
Pancakes with strawberries and cream.

Which do you like better: cats or dogs?
Dogs, of course. Cats are dumb. (Except for the smart ones.)

What do you value most in your friends?
That they laugh at my jokes. Even if they're not funny.

Where do you go for peace and quiet?
I close my eyes and concentrate on my breathing.

SQUARE FISH

What makes you laugh out loud?
Great comedy.

What's your favorite song?
Happy Birthday to you/You live in the zoo/You look like a monkey/
And you smell like one, too.

Who is your favorite fictional character?
Pinky Ponky, the shonky wonky bonky donkey.

What are you most afraid of?
Being chased around the bath by brown blobs.

What time of year do you like best?
Winter: It's much cozier to stay inside and write than in summer.

What's your favorite TV show?
Hannah Montana!

**If you were stranded on a desert island, who would you want
for company?**
My wife.

If you could travel in time, where would you go?
Back to prehistoric times to see dinosaurs fighting. That would
be cool.

**What's the best advice you have ever received about
writing?**
Write as fast as you can without stopping or thinking about what
you're writing. You can edit it later.

**What do you want readers to remember about your
books?**
That they had a great time!

What would you do if you ever stopped writing?
Start again.

What is your worst habit?
Laughing at my own jokes.

What do you consider to be your greatest accomplishment?
Getting other people to laugh at my jokes.

Where in the world do you feel most at home?
Wherever I happen to be. But especially at home. Duh!

What do you wish you could do better?
Fix things when they're broken.

What would your readers be most surprised to learn about you?
That I'm three billion years old. It's not true, but I think my readers would be quite surprised to learn about it if it was.

GOFISH

TERRY DENTON

What did you want to be when you grew up?
I guess I always dreamed of being an artist, but never really thought it would happen. I wanted to be an animator, as well. And a zookeeper.

When did you realize you wanted to be an artist?
When I really got serious about it was when I was about twenty-two at university. I was doing cartoons in the newspaper and thought "Wow! I can do this!"

What's your first childhood memory?
Coming with my mum to the new house we had just bought and looking through the big iron gates.

What's your most embarrassing childhood memory?
Wetting my pants at school in prep class.

What's your favorite childhood memory?
Waking up one Christmas morning and my cousin had bought us a blow-up swimming pool, and it was all set up with water in the back garden. I looked down on it from my bedroom and thought I was in heaven. [Christmas in Australia is in summer.]

As a young person, who did you look up to most?
Maybe my brothers. But my childhood was remarkably free of heroes.

What was your worst subject in school?
Singing! Definitely. Still is. Also physics in secondary school.

What was your best subject in school?
We didn't have art at our school. But that would have been. Other than that, chemistry and science, in general [except physics].

What was your first job?
Working at my dad's pharmacy. Counting out pills and doing deliveries.

How did you celebrate publishing your first book?
With a satisfied smile, and got on with the next one. I don't get that big a kick out of the publication. The bit I love is when I take the finished drawings to the publisher. We often have champagne. Then it takes another six months before the book is published. By then, I am on to something else.

Where do you find inspiration for your art?
Most inspiration comes from the world and people around me. Just observing the little things.

Are you a morning person or a night owl?
Bit of a night owl. But when I had young kids, I became a morning person. But the nighttime inspires me. Gets me thinking.

What's your idea of the best meal ever?
Lobster on holidays with my family when I was young.

Which do you like better: cats or dogs?
I like cats. They are so self-contained. Dogs annoy me. They are idiots. And they eat their own sick!

What do you value most in your friends?
Friendship is the great thing about humans. I just love spending time with friends doing nothing much. Just time spent.

Where do you go for peace and quiet?
I walk to the beach, which is close by. Or my block of land about five minutes away. Or a friend's farm where we go horse-riding.

What makes you laugh out loud?
Dogs eating their own sick. Stuff my kids say. About a hundred things a day.

What's your favorite song?
"Moon River" sung by Audrey Hepburn from *Breakfast at Tiffany's*.

Who is your favorite fictional character?
Philip Marlowe from the Raymond Chandler books.

What are you most afraid of?
Death. Only because I hate leaving with the story unfinished.

What time of year do you like best?
Summer in the sun and surf, by the beach, and down in the country.

What's your favorite TV show?
The West Wing, Cowboy Bebop, and *Father Ted.*

If you were stranded on a desert island, who would you want for company?
My friend Tim, but don't tell my wife. Tim and I would have fun making a boat and fishing and turn it into a Swiss Family Robinson event.

If you could travel in time, where would you go?
Maybe to 2070 to see what kind of world we have by then. And to see my kids grown up.

What's the best advice you have ever received about drawing?
Draw what you love drawing. And follow your instincts.

What would you do if you ever stopped drawing?
Decompose.

What do you like best about yourself?
That I care for people and that I <u>do</u> trust my instincts.

What is your worst habit?
Trying to do too much instead of having a bit of space in my day so I can think.

What do you consider to be your greatest accomplishment?
I guess when I see my kids; I think that is hard to beat.

Where in the world do you feel most at home?
At home. Where my family is. And there is a place 200 kilometers away from where I live that I often go to. A national park called Wilsons Promontory. And I feel very close to that.

What do you wish you could do better?
Sing!!!!!!!!!!

What would readers be most surprised to learn about you?
There is nothing surprising about me.

After reading this 99.9% fact-free book, no one will ever be able to stump you by pointing at a body part and demanding to know, "What body part is that?"

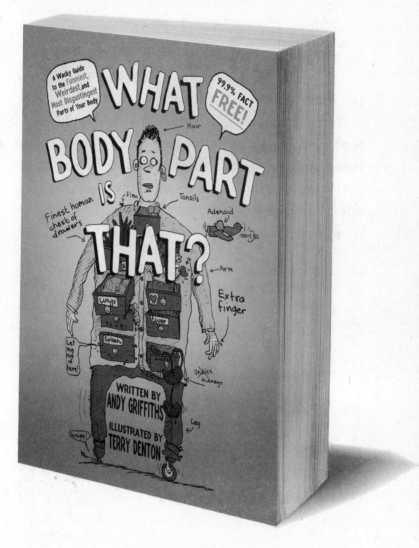

Turn the page to find out absolutely zip, zero, nada about the human body in

WHAT BODY PART IS THAT?

1. Head

Your head sits on top of your neck.

It has seven holes: two eye holes, two ear holes, two nose holes, and one cake hole.

You put pictures into your eye holes, sounds into your ear holes, air into your nose holes, and cakes into your cake hole. (You can also put a wide variety of healthy fresh fruits and vegetables into your cake hole, but I mostly use mine for cake.)

That is all there is to know about your head.

A&T'S FUN BODY PART FACT #1

In ancient times, there was a race of people who used to carry their heads under their arms.

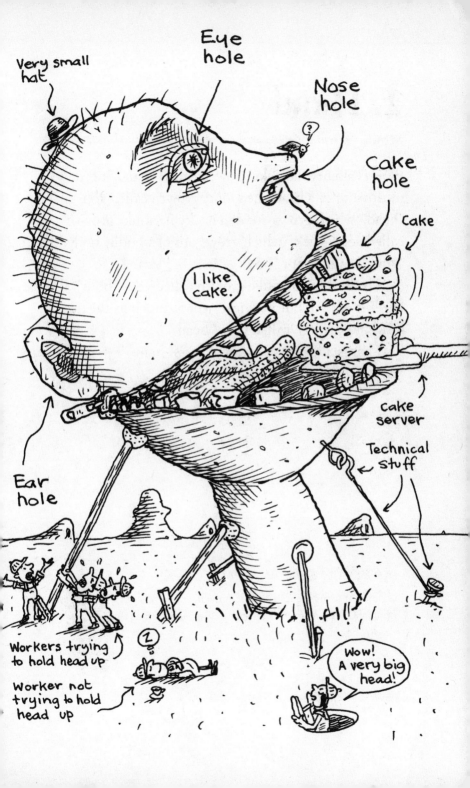

2. Hair

Hair is a hairy hair-like growth called "hair." It grows mostly out of a heady head-like growth called your "head," which grows out of a necky neck-like growth called your "neck," which grows out of a bodily body-like growth called your "body."

The bodily body-like growth called your "body" also has lots of hair, but nowhere near as much as the heady head-like growth called your "head."

That is all there is to know about hair.

A&T'S FUN BODY PART FACT #2

In ancient times, people used to grow their hair really long and wrap it around their bodies because clothes hadn't been invented yet.

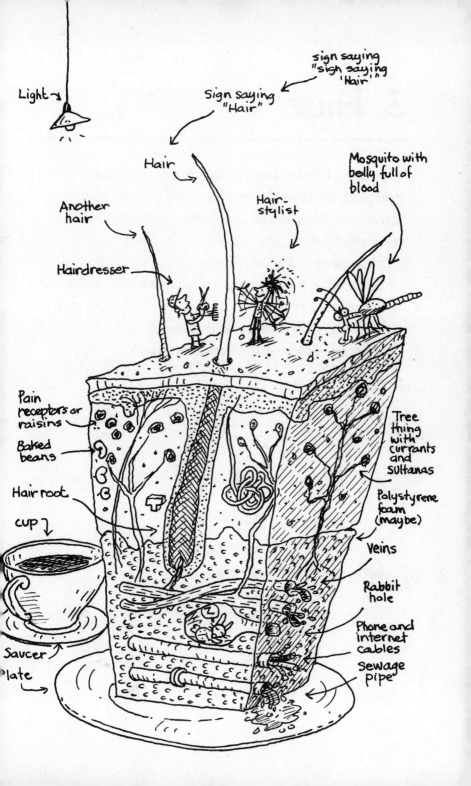

3. Face

Faces are a handy place on the front of the head to keep stuff like eyes, eyebrows, noses, mouths, cheeks, foreheads, chins, beards, and moustaches right where you need them.

Faces are not a good place to keep dirty socks and underpants, sporting equipment, apple cores, candy wrappers, and other bits of rubbish. (The proper place to keep this stuff is on your bedroom floor.)

That is all there is to know about faces.

A&T'S FUN BODY PART FACT #3

Every year in Australia, more than 300 people have their faces ripped off by killer koalas from outer space.

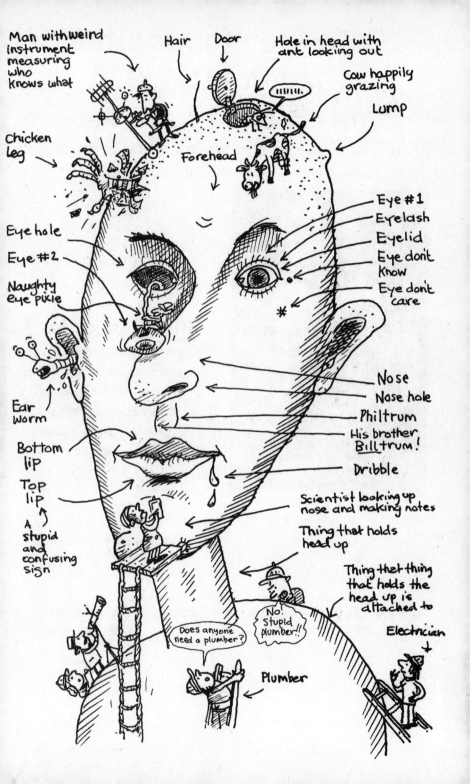

Get ready for another laugh attack!

The Cat on the Mat Is Flat

Written by Andy Griffiths; Illustrated by Terry Denton

978-0-312-53584-1 · $6.99 US / $8.99 Can.

Muck! Uck! Yuck!

It's just bad luck

when the truck of a duck

gets stuck in the muck.

Or when a dog on a cog

gets chased by a frog

around the bog of
an angry hog.

All of this and so much more!

We promise it won't
be a snore!

These wacky rhymes just
don't bore!

SQUARE FISH
WWW.SQUAREFISHBOOKS.COM
AVAILABLE WHEREVER BOOKS ARE SOLD